William Steig

WIZZIL

illustrated by Quentin Blake

PUFFIN

For Jane and Bob - W.S.

PUFFIN BOOKS

UK | USA | Canada | Ireland | Australia
India | New Zealand | South Africa

Puffin Books is part of the Penguin Random House group of companies
whose addresses can be found at global.penguinrandomhouse.com.

www.penguin.co.uk
www.puffin.co.uk
www.ladybird.co.uk

First published in the United States by Farrar Strauss Giroux 2000
Bloomsbury edition published 2002
Puffin edition 2017
001

Text copyright © William Steig, 2000
Illustrations copyright © Quentin Blake, 2000
The moral right of the author and illustrator has been asserted

Printed in China

A CIP catalogue record for this book is available from the British Library

ISBN: 978–0–141–37466-6

All correspondence to:
Puffin Books
Penguin Random House Children's
80 Strand, London WC2R 0RL

MIX
Paper from
responsible sources
FSC® C018179

Penguin Random House is committed to a
sustainable future for our business, our readers
and our planet. This book is made from Forest
Stewardship Council® certified paper.

Wizzil the witch was busy biting her nails. "Beatrice," she said,
"I'm bored stiff."

"Well, you've been perched on your behind for so long you're
stinking the place up," said the parrot. "Now, go make somebody suffer!"

"But who?" said Wizzil. "And where?"

"Frimp Farm," yapped Beatrice. "It's a Frimpy family, all right.
There's DeWitt Frimp, Fred Frimp, and Fred's wife, Florence Frimp."

Wizzil took her parrot's advice, turned herself into a common
housefly, and zizzled on over to Frimp Farm to check it out incognito.

Snoozing and snoring, with a flyswatter in his fist, was DeWitt
Frimp. He detested every breed of fly, especially *Musca domestica*.
And since he wasn't up to milking cows anymore, he had plenty of
time for swatting.

Wizzil lit on his bald pate, and acting like a genuine fly, she sallied down his nose, crossed his cheek, and tickled his ear with her tiny feet. DeWitt sprang up, swishing his swatter wherever he could swish it, three times missing the witch by only a hair.

Resolved on revenge, Wizzil zoomed out the window, determined to cook up a really nasty plan. "Wizzil," she said to herself, "that bald-headed fuddy-dud with his crazy swatter darn near did me in! He'll be getting his all right, and double-quick!"

Once she got home, Wizzil hurled her body onto her bed and stared
at the ceiling as if she dared it to try staring back.

Suddenly she got up and began pacing the floor in her snakeskin slippers. "Beatrice," said the witch, "listen. That old fogey keeps his swatter in his left hand, so he's a lefty."

"I'm going to turn myself into a left-handed work glove and
make sure he wears me constantly. Then I'll give him the works!"

"That's the way, Wizzil," Beatrice squawked. "Make him sizzle!"

Before sunrise the next day, Wizzil was down near the Frimp mailbox, skulking in the bushes. When the sun showed up, so did DeWitt, a flyswatter in his left hand and a letter in his right.

Presto! What had been a witch became a glove. After posting his letter, DeWitt spotted it.

"Frimp, my man, it's your lucky day!" he exclaimed, and he traipsed
back home with a happy harpy on his hand.

DeWitt took to wearing his new glove all the time, except when
he washed or shaved or had to wind his watch or pick his nose.
He wore it at breakfast, lunch and dinner, as if that was
normal behaviour.

Wizzil gave him time to get used to her, but then she got busy.
And DeWitt soon found himself losing his war on the flies. He'd swing
and he'd swat, and he'd hear the swatter swoosh, but Wizzil just
jerked his arm a tad to this side or a tad to that side . . . no soap!

This made DeWitt dippy sometimes – he'd let out a war cry and chase the little devils all over the house, hitting everything in sight. Except flies.

"Are you all right, Pops?" Florence Frimp finally asked.

"I'm fine as wine," DeWitt lied.

"Baloney," said Fred Frimp. "You've been acting nutty ever since you found that glove."

"Nutty? If anyone around here's nutty, it's you. Anyway, I won't stop wearing it."

"Please, Pops," said Florence. "Just take it off for one day and see what happens."

"No way, and that's that," he said.

But they kept pestering him until the witch lost patience and
decided to teach Fred and Florence to mind their own business.
She began by giving them unbearable itches in unexpected places,
and the harder they scratched, the more they itched.

At dinner that night she made their meatballs explode and their water spurt up like fountains.

And in the morning she made the whole house tremble and shake
so that the boards it was built with cried for help.

Making his sad way over the bridge that afternoon, having witnessed the weird things that were happening, DeWitt finally saw the light. Fred and Florence must be right. The glove had to be the culprit! He wrenched it from his wrist and flung it into the river.

Wizzil the glove began squirming and stretching and, right there in the water, began turning into the hateful hag she had always been.

And oh, how Wizzil hated getting wet (she'd never had a bath since
she was a helpless baby, and all she'd ever washed since then was
her two horrid hands). She thrashed, gurgled, spluttered and spat,
and then she started to sink.

DeWitt stared in disbelief, but repulsive as Wizzil was, DeWitt
couldn't bear to see a fellow creature drowning. He dived right in, and
holding the disgusting witch in his arms, he started towing her ashore.

Halfway there, he was startled to see that this witch, instead of looking sinister, was blushing. *Blushing!* And smiling with gratitude into his wide-open eyes.

Wizzil had been so thoroughly cleansed by the crystal-clear water that all her vicious nastiness was whirled away downstream.

Instead of running for his life as soon as they hit the riverbank,
DeWitt found himself hugging a surprisingly sweet old lady.

Needless to say, Wizzil and DeWitt fell completely in love, and
wound up an old married couple who stayed together on the farm.

Wizzil was never bored again. Sometimes she and DeWitt even played cards with Fred and Florence, and Beatrice would kibitz at their games.

"I guess I'll have to stay here with these humdrum humans," the parrot figured. "It'll be a whole new hayride."